The People of the Crater

Andre Alice Norton

About Norton:

Andre Alice Norton (February 17, 1912 – March 17, 2005), science fiction and fantasy author (with some works of historical fiction and contemporary fiction), was born Alice Mary Norton in Cleveland, Ohio, in the United States. She published her first novel in 1934. She was the first woman to receive the Gandalf Grand Master Award from the World Science Fiction Society in 1977, and she won the Damon Knight Memorial Grand Master Award from the SFWA in 1983. She wrote under the noms de plume Andre Norton, Andrew North and Allen Weston.

Transcriber's Note:

This etext was produced from *Fantasy Book* Vol. 1 number 1 (1947). Extensive research did not uncover any evidence that the U.S. copyright on this publication was renewed. Minor spelling and typographical errors have been corrected without note.

Chapter 1 Through the Blue Haze

Six months and three days after the Peace of Shanghai was signed and the great War of 1965-1970 declared at an end by an exhausted world, a young man huddled on a park bench in New York, staring miserably at the gravel beneath his badly worn shoes. He had been trained to fill the pilot's seat in the control cabin of a fighting plane and for nothing else. The search for a niche in civilian life had cost him both health and ambition.

A newcomer dropped down on the other end of the bench. The flyer studied him bitterly. *He* had decent shoes, a warm coat, and that air of satisfaction with the world which is the result of economic security. Although he was well into middle age, the man had a compact grace of movement and an air of alertness.

"Aren't you Captain Garin Featherstone?"

Startled, the flyer nodded dumbly.

From a plump billfold the man drew a clipping and waved it toward his seat mate. Two years before, Captain Garin Featherstone of the United Democratic Forces had led a perilous bombing raid into the wilds of Siberia to wipe out the vast expeditionary army secretly gathering there. It had been a spectacular affair and had brought the survivors some fleeting fame.

"You're the sort of chap I've been looking for," the stranger folded the clipping again, "a flyer with courage, initiative and brains. The man who led that raid is worth investing in."

"What's the proposition?" asked Featherstone wearily. He no longer believed in luck.

"I'm Gregory Farson," the other returned as if that should answer the question.

"The Antarctic man!"

"Just so. As you have probably heard, I was halted on the eve of my last expedition by the sudden spread of war to this country. Now I am preparing to sail south again."

"But I don't see—"

"How you can help me? Very simple, Captain Featherstone. I need pilots. Unfortunately the war has disposed of most of them. I'm lucky to contact one such as yourself—"

And it was as simple as that. But Garin didn't really believe that it was more than a dream until they touched the glacial shores of the polar continent some months later. As they brought ashore the three large planes, he began to wonder at the driving motive behind Farson's vague plans.

When the supply ship sailed, not to return for a year, Farson called them together. Three of the company were pilots, all war veterans, and two were engineers who spent most of their waking hours engrossed in the maps Farson produced.

"Tomorrow," the leader glanced from face to face, "we start inland. Here—" On a map spread before him he indicated a line marked in purple.

"Ten years ago I was a member of the Verdane expedition. Once, when flying due south, our plane was caught by some freakish air current and drawn off its course. When we were totally off our map, we saw in the distance a thick bluish haze. It seemed to rise in a straight line from the ice plain to the sky. Unfortunately our fuel was low and we dared not risk a closer investigation. So we fought our way back to the base.

"Verdane, however, had little interest in our report and we did not investigate it. Three years ago that Kattack expedition, hunting oil deposits by the order of the Dictator, reported seeing the same haze. This time we are going to explore it!"

"Why," Garin asked curiously, "are you so eager to penetrate this haze?—I gather that's what we're to do—"

Farson hesitated before answering. "It has often been suggested that beneath the ice sheeting of this continent may be hidden mineral wealth. I believe that the haze is caused by some form of volcanic activity, and perhaps a break in the crust."

Garin frowned at the map. He wasn't so sure about that explanation, but Farson was paying the bills. The flyer shrugged away his uneasiness. Much could be forgiven a man who allowed one to eat regularly again.

Four days later they set out. Helmly, one of the engineers, Rawlson, a pilot, and Farson occupied the first plane. The other engineer and pilot were in the second and Garin, with the extra supplies, was alone in the third.

He was content to be alone as they took off across the blue-white waste. His ship, because of its load, was loggy, so he did not attempt to follow the other two into the higher lane. They were in communication by radio and Garin, as he snapped on his earphones, remembered something Farson had said that morning:

"The haze affects radio. On our trip near it the static was very bad. Almost," with a laugh, "like speech in some foreign tongue."

As they roared over the ice Garin wondered if it might have been speech—from, perhaps, a secret enemy expedition, such as the Kattack one.

In his sealed cockpit he did not feel the bite of the frost and the ship rode smoothly. With a little sigh of content he settled back against the cushions, keeping to the course set by the planes ahead and above him.

Some five hours after they left the base, Garin caught sight of a dark shadow far ahead. At the same time Farson's voice chattered in his earphones.

"That's it. Set course straight ahead."

The shadow grew until it became a wall of purple-blue from earth to sky. The first plane was quite close to it, diving down into the vapor. Suddenly the ship rocked violently and swung earthward as if out of control. Then it straightened and turned back. Garin could hear Farson demanding to know what was the matter. But from the first plane there was no reply.

As Farson's plane kept going Garin throttled down. The actions of the first ship indicated trouble. What if that haze were a toxic gas?

"Close up, Featherstone!" barked Farson suddenly.

He obediently drew ahead until they flew wing to wing. The haze was just before them and now Garin could see movement in it, oily, impenetrable billows. The motors bit into it. There was clammy, foggy moisture on the windows.

Abruptly Garin sensed that he was no longer alone. Somewhere in the empty cabin behind him was another intelligence, a measuring power. He fought furiously against it—against the very idea of it. But, after a long, terrifying moment while it seemed to study him, it took control. His hands and feet still manipulated the ship, but *it* flew!

On the ship hurtled through the thickening mist. He lost sight of Farson's plane. And, though he was still fighting against the will which over-rode his, his struggles grew weaker. Then came the order to dive into the dark heart of the purple mists.

Down they whirled. Once, as the haze opened, Garin caught a glimpse of tortured gray rock seamed with yellow. Farson had been right: here the ice crust was broken.

Down and down. If his instruments were correct the plane was below sea level now. The haze thinned and was gone. Below spread a plain cloaked in vivid green. Here and there reared clumps of what might be trees. He saw, too, the waters of a yellow stream.

But there was something terrifyingly alien about that landscape. Even as he circled above it, Garin wrested to break the grip of the will that had brought him there. There came a crackle of sound in his earphones and at that moment the Presence withdrew.

The nose of the plane went up in obedience to his own desire. Frantically he climbed away from the green land. Again the haze absorbed him. He watched the moisture bead on the windows. Another hundred feet or so and he would be free of it—and that unbelievable world beneath.

Then, with an ominous sputter, the port engine conked out. The plane lurched and slipped into a dive. Down it whirled again into the steady light of the green land.

Trees came out of the ground, huge fern-like plants with crimson scaled trunks. Toward a clump of these the plane swooped.

Frantically Garin fought the controls. The ship steadied, the dive became a fast glide. He looked for an open space to land. Then he felt the landing gear scrape some surface. Directly ahead loomed one of the fern trees. The plane sped toward the long fronds. There came a ripping crash, the splintering of metal and wood. The scarlet cloud gathering before Garin's eyes turned black.

Chapter 2 The Folk of Tav

Garin returned to consciousness through a red mist of pain. He was pinned in the crumpled mass of metal which had once been the cabin. Through a rent in the wall close to his head thrust a long spike of green, shredded leaves still clinging to it. He lay and watched it, not daring to move lest the pain prove more than he could bear.

It was then that he heard the pattering sound outside. It seemed as if soft hands were pushing and pulling at the wreck. The tree branch shook and a portion of the cabin wall dropped away with a clang.

Garin turned his head slowly. Through the aperture was clambering a goblin figure.

It stood about five feet tall, and it walked upon its hind legs in human fashion, but the legs were short and stumpy, ending in feet with five toes of equal length. Slender, shapely arms possessed small hands with only four digits. The creature had a high, well-rounded forehead but no chin, the face being distinctly lizard-like in contour. The skin was a dull black, with a velvety surface. About its loins it wore a short kilt of metallic cloth, the garment being supported by a jeweled belt of exquisite workmanship.

For a long moment the apparition eyed Garin. And it was those golden eyes, fixed unwinkingly on his, which banished the flyer's fear. There was nothing but great pity in their depths.

The lizard-man stooped and brushed the sweat-dampened hair from Garin's forehead. Then he fingered the bonds of metal which held the flyer, as if estimating their strength. Having done so, he turned to the opening and apparently gave an order, returning again to squat by Garin.

Two more of his kind appeared to tear away the ruins of the cockpit. Though they were very careful, Garin fainted twice before they had freed him. He was placed on a litter swung between two clumsy beasts which might have been small elephants, except that they lacked trunks and possessed four tusks each.

They crossed the plain to the towering mouth of a huge cavern where the litter was taken up by four of the lizard-folk. The flyer lay staring up at the roof of the cavern. In the black stone had been carved fronds and flowers in bewildering profusion. Shining motes, giving off faint light, sifted through the air. At times as they advanced, these gathered in clusters and the light grew brighter.

Midway down a long corridor the bearers halted while their leader pulled upon a knob on the wall. An oval door swung back and the party passed through.

They came into a round room, the walls of which had been fashioned of creamy quartz veined with violet. At the highest point in the ceiling a large globe of the motes hung, furnishing soft light below.

Two lizard-men, clad in long robes, conferred with the leader of the flyer's party before coming to stand over Garin. One of the robed ones shook his head at the sight of the flyer's twisted body and waved the litter on into an inner chamber.

Here the walls were dull blue and in the exact center was a long block of quartz. By this the litter was put down and the bearers disappeared. With sharp knives the robed men cut away furs and leather to expose Garin's broken body.

They lifted him to the quartz table and there made him fast with metal bonds. Then one of them went to the wall and pulled a gleaming rod. From the dome of the roof shot an eerie blue light to beat upon Garin's helpless body. There followed a tingling through every muscle and joint, a prickling sensation in his skin, but soon his pain vanished as if it had never been.

The light flashed off and the three lizard-men gathered around him. He was wrapped in a soft robe and carried to another room. This, too, was circular, shaped like the half of a giant bubble. The floor sloped toward the center where there was a depression filled with cushions. There they laid Garin. At the top of the bubble, a pinkish cloud formed. He watched it drowsily until he fell asleep.

Something warm stirred against his bare shoulder. He opened his eyes, for a moment unable to remember where he was. Then there was a plucking at the robe twisted about him and he looked down.

If the lizard-folk had been goblin in their grotesqueness this visitor was elfin. It was about three feet high, its monkey-like body completely covered with silky white hair. The tiny hands were human in shape and hairless, but its feet were much like a cat's paws. From either side of the small round head branched large fan-shaped ears. The face was furred and boasted stiff cat whiskers on the upper lip. These *Anas*, as Garin learned later, were happy little creatures, each one choosing some mistress or master among the Folk, as this one had come to him. They were content to follow their big protector, speechless with delight at trifling gifts. Loyal and brave, they could do simple tasks or carry written messages for their chosen friend, and they remained with him until death. They were neither beast nor human, but rumored to be the result of some experiment carried out eons ago by the Ancient Ones.

After patting Garin's shoulder the Ana touched the flyer's hair wonderingly, comparing the bronze lengths with its own white fur. Since the Folk were hairless, hair was a strange sight in the Caverns. With a contented purr, it rubbed its head against his hand.

With a sudden click a door in the wall opened. The Ana got to its feet and ran to greet the newcomers. The chieftain of the Folk, he who had first discovered Garin, entered, followed by several of his fellows.

The flyer sat up. Not only was the pain gone but he felt stronger and younger than he had for weary months. Exultingly, he stretched wide his arms and grinned at the lizard-being who murmured happily in return.

Lizard-men busied themselves about Garin, girding on him the short kilt and jewel-set belt which were the only clothing of the Caverns. When they were finished, the chieftain took his hand and drew him to the door.

They traversed a hallway whose walls were carved and inlaid with glittering stones and metalwork, coming, at last, into a huge cavern, the outer walls of which were hidden by shadows. On a dais stood three tall thrones and Garin was conducted to the foot of these.

The highest throne was of rose crystal. On its right was one of green jade, worn smooth by centuries of time. At the left was the third, carved of a single block of jet. The rose throne and that of jet were unoccupied, but in the seat of jade reposed one of the Folk. He was taller than his fellows, and in his eyes, as he stared at Garin, was wisdom—and a brooding sadness.

"It is well!" The words resounded in the flyer's head. "We have chosen wisely. This youth is fit to mate with the Daughter. But he will be tried, as fire tries metal. He must win the Daughter forth and strive with Kepta—"

A hissing murmur echoed through the hall. Garin guessed that hundreds of the Folk must be gathered there.

"Urg!" the being on the throne commanded.

The chieftain moved a step toward the dais.

"Do you take this youth and instruct him. And then will I speak with him again. For—" sadness colored the words now—"we would have the rose throne filled again and the black one blasted into dust. Time moves swiftly."

The Chieftain led a wondering Garin away.

Chapter 3 Garin Hears of the Black Ones

Urg brought the flyer into one of the bubble-shaped rooms which contained a low, cushioned bench facing a metal screen—and here they seated themselves.

What followed was a language lesson. On the screen appeared objects which Urg would name, to have his sibilant uttering repeated by Garin. As the American later learned, the ray treatment he had undergone had quickened his mental powers, and in an incredibly short time he had a working vocabulary.

Judging by the pictures the lizard folk were the rulers of the crater world, although there were other forms of life there. The elephant-like *Tand* was a beast of burden, the squirrel-like *Eron* lived underground and carried on a crude agriculture in small clearings, coming shyly twice a year to exchange grain for a liquid rubber produced by the Folk.

Then there was the *Gibi*, a monstrous bee, also friendly to the lizard people. It supplied the cavern dwellers with wax, and in return the Folk gave the Gibi colonies shelter during the unhealthful times of the Great Mists.

Highly civilized were the Folk. They did no work by hand, except the finer kinds of jewel setting and carving. Machines wove their metal cloth, machines prepared their food, harvested their fields, hollowed out new dwellings.

Freed from manual labor they had turned to acquiring knowledge. Urg projected on the screen pictures of vast laboratories and great libraries of scientific lore. But all they knew in the beginning, they had learned from the Ancient Ones, a race unlike themselves, which had preceded them in sovereignty over *Tav*. Even the Folk themselves were the result of constant forced evolution and experimentation carried on by these Ancient Ones.

All this wisdom was guarded most carefully, but against what or whom, Urg could not tell, although he insisted that the danger was very real. There was something within the blue wall of the crater which disputed the Folk's rule.

As Garin tried to probe further a gong sounded. Urg arose.

"It is the hour of eating," he announced. "Let us go."

They came to a large room where a heavy table of white stone stretched along three walls, benches before it. Urg seated himself and pressed a knob on the table, motioning Garin to do likewise. The wall facing them opened and two trays slid out. There was a platter of hot meat covered with rich sauce, a stone bowl of grain porridge and a cluster of fruit, still fastened to a leafy branch. This the Ana eyed so wistfully that Garin gave it to the creature.

The Folk ate silently and arose quietly when they had finished, their trays vanishing back through the wall. Garin noticed only males in the room and recalled that he had, as yet, seen no females among the Folk. He ventured a question.

Urg chuckled. "So, you think there are no women in the Caverns? Well, we shall go to the Hall of Women that you may see."

To the Hall of Women they went. It was breath-taking in its richness, stones worth a nation's ransom sparkling from its domed roof and painted walls. Here were the matrons and maidens of the Folk, their black forms veiled in robes of silver net, each cross strand of which was set with a tiny gem, so that they appeared to be wrapped in glittering scales.

There were not many of them—a hundred perhaps. And a few led by the hand smaller editions of themselves, who stared at Garin with round yellow eyes and chewed black fingertips shyly.

The women were intrusted with the finest jewel work, and with pride they showed the stranger their handiwork. At the far end of the hall was a wonderous thing in the making. One of the silver nets, which were the foundations of their robes, was fastened there and three of the women were putting small rose jewels into each microscopic setting. Here and there they had varied the pattern with tiny emeralds or flaming opals, so that the finished portion was a rainbow.

One of the workers smoothed the robe and glanced up at Garin, a gentle teasing in her voice as she explained:

"This is for the Daughter when she comes to her throne."

The Daughter! What had the Lord of the Folk said? "This youth is fit to mate with the Daughter." But Urg had said that the Ancient Ones had gone from Tav.

"Who is the Daughter?" he demanded.

"Thrala of the Light."

"Where is she?"

The woman shivered and there was fear in her eyes. "Thrala lies in the Caves of Darkness."

"The Caves of Darkness!" Did she mean Thrala was dead?

Was he, Garin Featherstone, to be the victim of some rite of sacrifice which was designed to unite him with the dead?

Urg touched his arm. "Not so. Thrala has not yet entered the Place of Ancestors."

"You know my thoughts?"

Urg laughed. "Thoughts are easy to read. Thrala lives. Sera served the Daughter as handmaiden while she was yet among us. Sera, do you show us Thrala as she was."

The woman crossed to a wall where there was a mirror such as Urg had used for his language lesson. She gazed into it and then beckoned the flyer to stand beside her.

The mirror misted and then he was looking, as if through a window, into a room with walls and ceiling of rose quartz. On the floor were thick rugs of silver rose. And a great heap of cushions made a low couch in the center.

"The inner chamber of the Daughter," Sera announced.

A circular panel in the wall opened and a woman slipped through. She was very young, little more than a girl. There were happy curves in her full crimson lips, joyous lights in her violet eyes.

She was human of shape, but her beauty was unearthly. Her skin was pearl white and other colors seemed to play faintly upon it, so that it reminded Garin of mother-of-pearl with its lights and shadows. The hair, which veiled her as a cloud, was blue-black and reached below her knees. She was robed in the silver net of the Folk and there was a heavy girdle of rose-shaded jewels about her slender waist.

"That was Thrala before the Black Ones took her," said Sera.

Garin uttered a cry of disappointment as the picture vanished. Urg laughed.

"What care you for shadows when the Daughter herself waits for you? You have but to bring her from the Caves of Darkness—"

"Where are these Caves—" Garin's question was interrupted by the pealing of the Cavern gong. Sera cried out:

"The Black Ones!"

Urg shrugged. "When they spared not the Ancient Ones how could we hope to escape? Come, we must go to the Hall of Thrones."

Before the jade throne of the Lord of the Folk stood a small group of the lizard-men beside two litters. As Garin entered the Lord spoke.

"Let the outlander come hither that he may see the work of the Black Ones."

Garin advanced unwillingly, coming to stand by those struggling things which gasped their message between moans and screams of agony. They were men of the Folk but their black skins were green with rot.

The Lord leaned forward on his throne. "It is well," he said. "You may depart."

As if obeying his command, the tortured things let go of the life to which they had clung and were still.

"Look upon the work of the Black Ones," the ruler said to Garin. "Jiv and Betv were captured while on a mission to the Gibi of the Cliff. It seems that the Black Ones needed material for their laboratories. They seek even to give the Daughter to their workers of horror!"

A terrible cry of hatred arose from the hall, and Garin's jaw set. To give that fair vision he had just seen to such a death as this—!

"Jiv and Betv were imprisoned close to the Daughter and they heard the threats of Kepta. Our brothers, stricken with foul disease, were sent forth to carry the plague to us, but they swam through the pool of boiling mud. They have died, but the evil died with them. And I think that while we breed such as they, the Black Ones shall not rest easy. Listen now, outlander, to the story of the Black Ones and the Caves of Darkness, of how the Ancient Ones brought the Folk up from the slime of a long dried sea and made them great, and of how the Ancient Ones at last went down to their destruction."

Chapter 4 The Defeat of the Ancient Ones

"In the days before the lands of the outer world were born of the sea, before even the Land of the Sun (Mu) and the Land of the Sea (Atlantis) arose from molten rock and sand, there was land here in the far south. A sere land of rock plains, and swamps where slimy life mated, lived and died.

"Then came the Ancient Ones from beyond the stars. Their race was already older than this earth. Their wise men had watched its birth-rending from the sun. And when their world perished, taking most of their blood into nothingness, a handful fled hither.

"But when they climbed from their space ship it was into hell. For they had gained, in place of their loved home, bare rock and stinking slime.

"They blasted out this Tav and entered into it with the treasures of their flying ships and also certain living creatures captured in the swamps. From these, they produced the Folk, the Gibi, the Tand, and the land-tending Eron.

"Among these, the Folk were eager for wisdom and climbed high. But still the learning of the Ancient Ones remained beyond their grasp.

"During the eons the Ancient Ones dwelt within their protecting wall of haze the outer world changed. Cold came to the north and south; the Land of Sun and the Land of Sea arose to bear the foot of true man. On their mirrors of seeing the Ancient Ones watched man-life spread across the world. They had the power of prolonging life, but still the race was dying. From without must come new blood. So certain men were summoned from the Land of the Sun. Then the race flourished for a space.

"The Ancient Ones decided to leave Tav for the outer world. But the sea swallowed the Land of Sun. Again, in the time of the Land of Sea, the stock within Tav was replenished and the Ancient Ones prepared for exodus; again the sea cheated them.

"Those men left in the outer world reverted to savagery. Since the Ancient Ones would not mingle their blood with that of almost beasts, they built the haze wall stronger and remained. But a handful of them were attracted by the forbidden, and secretly they summoned the beast men. Of that monstrous mating came the Black Ones. They live but for the evil they may do, and the power which they acquired is debased and used to forward cruelty.

"At first their sin was not discovered. When it was, the others would have slain the offspring but for the law which forbids them to kill. They must use their power for good or it departs from them. So they drove the Black Ones to the southern end of Tav and gave them the Caves of Darkness. Never were the Black Ones to come north of the River of Gold—nor were the Ancient Ones to go south of it.

"For perhaps two thousand years the Black Ones kept the law. But they worked, building powers of destruction. While matters rested thus, the Ancient Ones searched the world, seeking men by whom they could renew the race. Once there came men from an island far to the north. Six lived to penetrate the mists and take wives among the Daughters. Again, they called the yellow-haired men of another breed, great sea rovers.

"But the Black Ones called too. As the Ancient Ones searched for the best, the Black Ones brought in great workers of evil. And, at last, they succeeded in shutting off the channels of sending thought so that the Ancient Ones could call no more.

"Then did the Black Ones cross the River of Gold and enter the land of the Ancient Ones. Thran, Dweller in the Light and Lord of the Caverns, summoned the Folk to him.

"'There will come one to aid you,' he told us. 'Try the summoning again after the Black Ones have seemed to win. Thrala, Daughter of the Light, will not enter into the Room of Pleasant Death with the rest of the women, but will give herself into the hands of the Black Ones, that they may think themselves truly victorious. You of the Folk withdraw into the Place of Reptiles until the Black Ones are gone. Nor will all the Ancient Ones perish—more will be saved, but the manner of their preservation I dare not tell. When the sun-haired youth comes from the outer world, send him into the Caves of Darkness to rescue Thrala and put an end to evil.'

"And then the Lady Thrala arose and said softly, 'As the Lord Thran has said, so let it be. I shall deliver myself into the hands of the Black Ones that their doom may come upon them.'

"Lord Thran smiled upon her as he said: 'So will happiness be your portion. After the Great Mists, does not light come again?'

"The women of the Ancient Ones then took their leave and passed into the place of Pleasant Death while the men made ready for battle with the Black Ones. For three days they fought, but a new weapon of the Black Ones won the day, and the chief of the Black

Ones set up this throne of jet as proof of his power. Since, however, the Black Ones were not happy in the Caverns, longing for the darkness of their caves, they soon withdrew and we, the Folk, came forth again.

"But now the time has come when the dark ones will sacrifice the Daughter to their evil. If you can win her free, outlander, they shall perish as if they had not been."

"What of the Ancient Ones?" asked Garin—"those others Thran said would be saved?"

"Of those we know nothing save that when we bore the bodies of the fallen to the Place of Ancestors there were some missing. That you may see the truth of this story, Urg will take you to the gallery above the Room of Pleasant Death and you may look upon those who sleep there."

Urg guiding, Garin climbed a steep ramp leading from the Hall of Thrones. This led to a narrow balcony, one side of which was clear crystal. Urg pointed down.

They were above a long room whose walls were tinted jade green. On the polished floor were scattered piles of cushions. Each was occupied by a sleeping woman and several of these clasped a child in their arms. Their long hair rippled to the floor, their curved lashes made dark shadows on pale faces.

"But they are sleeping!" protested Garin.

Urg shook his head. "It is the sleep of death. Twice each ten hours vapors rise from the floor. Those breathing them do not wake again, and if they are undisturbed they will lie thus for a thousand years. Look there—"

He pointed to the closed double doors of the room. There lay the first men of the Ancient Ones Garin had seen. They, too, seemed but asleep, their handsome heads pillowed on their arms.

"Thran ordered those who remained after the last battle in the Hall of Thrones to enter the Room of Pleasant Death that the Black Ones might not torture them for their beastly pleasures. Thran himself remained behind to close the door, and so died."

There were no aged among the sleepers. None of the men seemed to count more than thirty years and many of them appeared younger. Garin remarked upon this.

"The Ancient Ones appeared thus until the day of their death, though many lived twice a hundred years. The light rays kept them so. Even we of the Folk can hold back age. But come now, our Lord

Trar would speak with you again."

Chapter 5 Into the Caves of Darkness

Again Garin stood before the jade throne of Trar and heard the stirring of the multitude of the Folk in the shadows. Trar was turning a small rod of glittering, greenish metal around in his soft hands.

"Listen well, outlander," he began, "for little time remains to us. Within seven days the Great Mists will be upon us. Then no living thing may venture forth from shelter and escape death. And before that time Thrala must be out of the Caves. This rod will be your weapon; the Black Ones have not its secret. Watch."

Two of the Folk dragged an ingot of metal before him. He touched it with the rod. Great flakes of rust appeared to spread across the entire surface. It crumpled away and one of the Folk trod upon the pile of dust where it had been.

"Thrala lies in the heart of the Caves but Kepta's men have grown careless with the years. Enter boldly and trust to fortune. They know nothing of your coming or of Thran's words concerning you."

Urg stood forward and held out his hands in appeal.

"What would you, Urg?"

"Lord, I would go with the outlander. He knows nothing of the Forest of the Morgels or of the Pool of Mud. It is easy to go astray in the woodland—"

Trar shook his head. "That may not be. He must go alone, even as Thran said."

The Ana, which had followed in Garin's shadow all day, whistled shrilly and stood on tiptoe to tug at his hand. Trar smiled. "That one may go, its eyes may serve you well. Urg will guide you to the outer portal of the Place of Ancestors and set you upon the road to the Caves. Farewell, outlander, and may the spirits of the Ancient Ones be with you."

Garin bowed to the ruler of the Folk and turned to follow Urg. Near the door stood a small group of women. Sera pressed forward from them, holding out a small bag.

"Outlander," she said hurriedly, "when you look upon the Daughter speak to her of Sera, for I have awaited her many years."

He smiled. "That I will."

"If you remember, outlander. I am a great lady among the

Folk and have my share of suitors, yet I think I could envy the Daughter. Nay, I shall not explain that," she laughed mockingly. "You will understand in due time. Here is a packet of food. Now go swiftly that we may have you among us again before the Mists."

So a woman's farewell sped them on their way. Urg chose a ramp which led downward. At its foot was a niche in the rock, above which a rose light burned dimly. Urg reached within the hollow and drew out a pair of high buskins which he aided Garin to lace on. They were a good fit, having been fashioned for a man of the Ancient Ones.

The passage before them was narrow and crooked. There was a thick carpet of dust underfoot, patterned by the prints of the Folk. They rounded a corner and a tall door loomed out of the gloom. Urg pressed the surface, there was a click and the stone rolled back.

"This is the Place of Ancestors," he announced as he stepped within.

They were at the end of a colossal hall whose domed roof disappeared into shadows. Thick pillars of gleaming crystal divided it into aisles, all leading inward to a raised dais of oval shape. Filling the aisles were couches and each soft nest held its sleeper. Near to the door lay the men and women of the Folk, but closer to the dais were the Ancient Ones. Here and there a couch bore a double burden, upon the shoulder of a man was pillowed the drooping head of a woman. Urg stopped beside such a one.

"See, outlander, here was one who was called from your world. Marena of the House of Light looked with favor upon him and their days of happiness were many."

The man on the couch had red-gold hair and on his upper arm was a heavy band of gold whose mate Garin had once seen in a museum. A son of pre-Norman Ireland. Urg traced with a crooked finger the archaic lettering carved upon the stone base of the couch.

"Lovers in the Light sleep sweetly. The Light returns on the appointed day."

"Who lies there?" Garin motioned to the dais.

"The first Ancient Ones. Come, look upon those who made this Tav."

On the dais the couches were arranged in two rows and between them, in the center, was a single couch raised above the others. Fifty men and women lay as if but resting for the hour, smiles on their peaceful faces but weary shadows beneath their eyes. There was an un-human quality about them which was lacking in their descendents.

Urg advanced to the high couch and beckoned Garin to join him. A man and a woman lay there, the woman's head upon the man's breast. There was that in their faces which made Garin turn away. He felt as if he had intruded roughly where no man should go.

"Here lies Thran, Son of Light, first Lord of the Caverns, and his lady Thrala, Dweller in the Light. So have they lain a thousand thousand years, and so will they lie until this planet rots to dust beneath them. They led the Folk out of the slime and made Tav. Such as they we shall never see again."

They passed silently down the aisles of the dead. Once Garin caught sight of another fair-haired man, perhaps another outlander, since the Ancient Ones were all dark of hair. Urg paused once more before they left the hall. He stood by the couch of a man, wrapped in a long robe, whose face was ravaged with marks of agony.

Urg spoke a single name: "Thran."

So this was the last Lord of the Caverns. Garin leaned closer to study the dead face but Urg seemed to have lost his patience. He hurried his charge on to a panel door.

"This is the southern portal of the Caverns," he explained. "Trust to the Ana to guide you and beware of the boiling mud. Should the morgels scent you, kill quickly, they are the servants of the Black Ones. May fortune favor you, outlander."

The door was open and Garin looked out upon Tav. The soft blue light was as strong as it had been when he had first seen it. With the Ana perched on his shoulder, the green rod and the bag of food in his hands, he stepped out onto the moss sod.

Urg raised his hand in salute and the door clicked into place. Garin stood alone, pledged to bring the Daughter out of the Caves of Darkness.

There is no night or day in Tav since the blue light is steady. But the Folk divide their time by artificial means. However Garin, being newly come from the rays of healing, felt no fatigue. As he hesitated, the Ana chattered and pointed confidently ahead.

Before them was a dense wood of fern trees. It was quiet in the forest as Garin made his way into its gloom and for the first time he noted a peculiarity of Tav. There were no birds.

The portion of the woodland they had to traverse was but a spur of the forest to the west. After an hour of travel they came out upon the bank of a sluggish river. The turbid waters of the stream were a dull saffron color. This, thought Garin, must be the River of Gold, the boundary of the lands of the Black Ones.

He rounded a bend to come upon a bridge, so old that time itself had worn its stone angles into curves. The bridge gave on a wide plain where tall grass grew sere and yellow. To the left was a hissing and bubbling, and a huge wave of boiling mud arose in the air. Garin choked in a wind, thick with chemicals, which blew from it. He smelled and tasted the sulphur-tainted air all across the plain.

And he was glad enough to plunge into a small fern grove which half-concealed a spring. There he bathed his head and arms while the Ana pulled open Sera's food bag.

Together they ate the cakes of grain and the dried fruit. When they were done the Ana tugged at Garin's hand and pointed on.

Cautiously Garin wormed his way through the thick underbrush until, at last, he looked out into a clearing and at its edge the entrance of the Black Ones' Caves. Two tall pillars, carved into the likeness of foul monsters, guarded a rough-edged hole. A fine greenish mist whirled and danced in its mouth.

The flyer studied the entrance. There was no life to be seen. He gripped the destroying rod and inched forward. Before the green mist he braced himself and then stepped within.

Chapter 6 Kepta's Second Prisoner

The green mist enveloped Garin. He drew into his lungs hot moist air faintly tinged with a scent of sickly sweetness, as from some hidden corruption. Green motes in the air gave forth little light and seemed to cling to the intruder.

With the Ana pattering before him, the American started down a steep ramp, the soft soles of his buskins making no sound. At regular intervals along the wall, niches held small statues. And about each perverted figure was a crown of green motes.

The Ana stopped, its large ears outspread as if to catch the faintest murmur of sound. From somewhere under the earth came the howls of a maddened dog. The Ana shivered, creeping closer to Garin.

Down led the ramp, growing narrower and steeper. And louder sounded the insane, coughing howls of the dog. Then the passage was abruptly barred by a grill of black stone. Garin peered through its bars at a flight of stairs leading down into a pit. From the pit arose snarling laughter.

Padding back and forth were things which might have been conceived by demons. They were sleek, rat-like creatures, hairless, and large as ponies. Red saliva dripped from the corners of their sharp jaws. But in the eyes, which they raised now and then toward the grill, there was intelligence. These were the morgels, watchdogs and slaves of the Black Ones.

From a second pair of stairs directly across the pit arose a moaning call. A door opened and two men came down the steps. The morgels surged forward, but fell back when whips were cracked over their heads.

The masters of the morgels were human in appearance. Black loin cloths were twisted about them and long, wing-shaped cloaks hung from their shoulders. On their heads, completely masking their hair, were cloth caps which bore ragged crests not unlike cockscombs. As far as Garin could see they were unarmed except for their whips.

A second party was coming down the steps. Between two of the Black Ones struggled a prisoner. He made a desperate and hopeless fight of it, but they dragged him to the edge of the pit before they halted. The morgels, intent upon their promised prey, crouched before them.

Five steps above were two figures to whom the guards looked for instructions. One was a man of their race, of slender, handsome body and evil, beautiful face. His hand lay possessively upon the arm of his companion.

It was Thrala who stood beside him, her head proudly erect. The laughter curves were gone from her lips; there was only sorrow and resignation to be read there now. But her spirit burned like a white flame in her eyes.

"Look!" her warder ordered. "Does not Kepta keep his promises? Shall we give Dandtan into the jaws of our slaves, or will you unsay certain words of yours, Lady Thrala?"

The prisoner answered for her. "Kepta, son of vileness, Thrala is not for you. Remember, beloved one," he spoke to the Daughter, "the day of deliverance is at hand—"

Garin felt a sudden emptiness. The prisoner had called Thrala "beloved" with the ease of one who had the right.

"I await Thrala's answer," Kepta returned evenly. And her answer he got.

"Beast among beasts, you may send Dandtan to his death, you may heap all manner of insult and evil upon me, but still I say the Daughter is not for your touch. Rather will I cut the line of life with my own hands, taking upon me the punishment of the Elder Ones. To Dandtan," she smiled down upon the prisoner, "I say farewell. We shall meet again beyond the Curtain of Time." She held out her hands to him.

"Thrala, dear one—!" One of his guards slapped a hand over the prisoner's mouth putting an end to his words.

But now Thrala was looking beyond him, straight at the grill which sheltered Garin. Kepta pulled at her arm to gain her attention. "Watch! Thus do my enemies die. To the pit with him!"

The guards twisted their prisoner around and the morgels crept closer, their eyes fixed upon that young, writhing body. Garin knew that he must take a hand in the game. The Ana was tugging him to the right, and there was an open archway leading to a balcony running around the side of the pit.

Those below were too entranced by the coming sport to notice the invader. But Thrala glanced up and Garin thought that she sighted him. Something in her attitude attracted Kepta, he too looked up. For a moment he stared in stark amazement, and then he thrust the Daughter through the door behind him.

"Ho, outlander! Welcome to the Caves. So the Folk have meddled—"

"Greeting, Kepta." Garin hardly knew whence came the words which fell so easily from his tongue. "I have come as was promised, to remain until the Black Throne is no more."

"Not even the morgels boast before their prey lies limp in their jaws," flashed Kepta. "What manner of beast are you?"

"A clean beast, Kepta, which you are not. Bid your two-legged morgels loose the youth, lest I grow impatient." The flyer swung the green rod into view.

Kepta's eyes narrowed but his smile did not fade. "I have heard of old that the Ancient Ones do not destroy—"

"As an outlander I am not bound by their limits," returned Garin, "as you will learn if you do not call off your stinking pack."

The master of the Caves laughed. "You are as the Tand, a fool without a brain. Never shall you see the Caverns again—"

"You shall own me master yet, Kepta."

The Black Chief seemed to consider. Then he waved to his men. "Release him," he ordered. "Outlander, you are braver than I thought. We might bargain—"

"Thrala goes forth from the Caves and the black throne is dust, those are the terms of the Caverns."

"And if we do not accept?"

"Then Thrala goes forth, the throne is dust and Tav shall have a day of judging such as it has never seen before."

"You challenge me?"

Again words, which seemed to Garin to have their origin elsewhere, came to him. "As in Yu-Lac, I shall take—"

Before Kepta could reply there was trouble in the pit. Dandtan, freed by his guards, was crossing the floor in running leaps. Garin threw himself belly down on the balcony and dropped the jeweled strap of his belt over the lip.

A moment later it snapped taut and he stiffened to an upward pull. Already Dandtan's heels were above the snapping jaws of a morgel. The flyer caught the youth around the shoulders and heaved. They rolled together against the wall.

"They are gone! All of them!" Dandtan cried, as he regained his feet. He was right; the morgels howled below, but Kepta and his men had vanished.

"Thrala!" Garin exclaimed.

Dandtan nodded. "They have taken her back to the cells. They believe her safe there."

"Then they think wrong." Garin stooped to pick up the green rod. His companion laughed.

"We'd best start before they get prepared for us."

Garin picked up the Ana. "Which way?"

Dandtan showed him a passage leading from behind the other door. Then he dodged into a side chamber to return with two of the wing cloaks and cloth hoods, so that they might pass as Black Ones.

They went by the mouths of three side tunnels, all deserted. None disputed their going. All the Black Ones had withdrawn from this part of the Caves.

Dandtan sniffed uneasily. "All is not well. I fear a trap."

"While we can pass, let us."

The passage curved to the right and they came into an oval room. Again Dandtan shook his head but ventured no protest. Instead he flung open a door and hurried down a short hall.

It seemed to Garin that there were strange rustlings and squeakings in the dark corners. Then Dandtan stopped so short that the flyer ran into him.

"Here is the guard room—and it is empty!"

Garin looked over his shoulder into a large room. Racks of strange weapons hung on the walls and the sleeping pallets of the guards were stacked evenly, but the men were nowhere to be seen.

They crossed the room and passed beneath an archway.

"Even the bars are not down," observed Dandtan. He pointed overhead. There hung a portcullis of stone. Garin studied it apprehensively. But Dandtan drew him on into a narrow corridor where were barred doors.

"The cells," he explained, and withdrew a bar across one door. The portal swung back and they pushed within.

Chapter 7 Kepta's Trap

Thrala arose to face them. Forgetting the disguise he wore, Garin drew back, chilled by her icy demeanor. But Dandtan sprang forward and caught her in his arms. She struggled madly until she saw the face beneath her captor's hood, and then she gave a cry of delight and her arms were about his neck.

"Dandtan!"

He smiled. "Even so. But it is the outlander's doing."

She came to the American, studying his face. "Outlander? So cold a name is not for you, when you have served us so." She offered him her hands and he raised them to his lips.

"And how are you named?"

Dandtan laughed. "Thus the eternal curiosity of women!"

"Garin."

"Garin," she repeated. "How like—" A faint rose glowed beneath her pearl flesh.

Dandtan's hand fell lightly upon his rescuer's shoulder. "Indeed he is like him. From this day let him bear that other's name. Garan, Son of Light."

"Why not?" she returned calmly. "After all—"

"The reward which might have been Garan's may be his? Tell him the story of his namesake when we are again in the Caverns—"

Dandtan was interrupted by a frightened squeak from the Ana. Then came a mocking voice.

"So the prey has entered the trap of its own will. How many hunters may boast the same?"

Kepta leaned against the door, the light of vicious mischief dancing in his eyes. Garin dropped his cloak to the floor, but Dandtan must have read what was in the flyer's mind, for he caught him by the arm.

"On your life, touch him not!"

"So you have learned that much wisdom while you have dwelt among us, Dandtan? Would that Thrala had done the same. But fair women find me weak." He eyed her proud body in a way that would have sent Garin at his throat had Dandtan not held him. "So shall Thrala have a second chance. How would you like to see these men in the Room of Instruments, Lady?"

"I do not fear you," she returned. "Thran once made a

prophecy, and he never spoke idly. We shall win free—"

"That will be as fate would have it. Meanwhile, I leave you to each other." He whipped around the door and slammed it behind him. They heard the grating of the bar he slid into place. Then his footsteps died away.

"There goes evil," murmured Thrala softly. "Perhaps it would have been better if Garin had killed him as he thought to do. We must get away... ."

Garin drew the rod from his belt. The green light-motes gathered and clung about its polished length.

"Touch not the door," Thrala advised; "only its hinges."

Beneath the tip of the rod the stone became spongy and flaked away. Dandtan and the flyer caught the door and eased it to the floor. With one quick movement Thrala caught up Garin's cloak and swirled it about her, hiding the glitter of her gem-encrusted robe.

There was a curious cold lifelessness about the air of the corridor, the light-bearing motes vanishing as if blown out.

"Hurry!" the Daughter urged. "Kepta is withdrawing the living light, so that we will have to wander in the dark."

When they reached the end of the hall the light was quite gone, and Garin bruised his hands against the stone portcullis which had been lowered. From somewhere on the other side of the barrier came rippling laughter.

"Oh, outlander," called Kepta mockingly, "you will get through easily enough when you remember your weapon. But the dark you can not conquer so easily, nor that which runs the halls."

Garin was already busy with the rod. Within five minutes their way was clear again. But Thrala stopped them when they would have gone through. "Kepta has loosed the hunters."

"The hunters?"

"The morgels and—others," explained Dandtan. "The Black Ones have withdrawn and only death comes this way. And the morgels see in the dark... ."

"So does the Ana."

"Well thought of," agreed the son of the Ancient Ones.
"It will lead us out."

As if in answer, there came a tug at Garin's belt. Reaching back, he caught Thrala's hand and knew that she had taken Dandtan's. So linked they crossed the guard room. Then the Ana paused for a long time, as if listening. There was nothing to see but the darkness which hung about them like the smothering folds of a curtain.

"Something follows us," whispered Dandtan.

"Nothing to fear," stated Thrala. "It dare not attack. It is, I think, of Kepta's fashioning. And that which has not true life dreads death above all things. It is going—"

There came sounds of something crawling slowly away.

"Kepta will not try that again," continued the Daughter, disdainfully. "He knew that his monstrosities would not attack. Only in the light are they to be dreaded—and then only because of the horror of their forms."

Again the Ana tugged at its master's belt. They shuffled into the narrow passage beyond. But there remained the sense of things about them in the dark, things which Thrala continued to insist were harmless and yet which filled Garin with loathing.

Then they entered the far corridor into which led the three halls and which ended in the morgel pit. Here, Garin believed, was the greatest danger from the morgels.

The Ana stopped short, dropping back against Garin's thigh. In the blackness appeared two yellow disks, sparks of saffron in their depths. Garin thrust the rod into Thrala's hands.

"What do you?" she demanded.

"I'm going to clear the way. It's too dark to use the rod against moving creatures... ." He flung the words over his shoulder as he moved toward the unwinking eyes.

Chapter 8 Escape from the Caves

Keeping his eyes upon those soulless yellow disks, Garin snatched off his hood, wadding it into a ball. Then he sprang. His fingers slipped on smooth hide, sharp fangs ripped his forearm, blunt nails scraped his ribs. A foul breath puffed into his face and warm slaver trickled down his neck and chest. But his plan succeeded.

The cap was wedged into the morgel's throat and the beast was slowly choking. Blood dripped from the flyer's torn flesh, but he held on grimly until he saw the light fade from those yellow eyes. The dying morgel made a last mad plunge for freedom, dragging his attacker along the rock floor. Then Garin felt the heaving body rest limply against his own. He staggered against the wall, panting.

"Garin!" cried Thrala. Her questing hand touched his shoulder and crept to his face. "It is well with you?"

"Yes," he panted, "let us go on."

Thrala's fingers had lingered on his arm and now she walked beside him, her cloak making whispering sounds as it brushed against the wall and floor.

"Wait," she cautioned suddenly. "The morgel pit… ."

Dandtan slipped by them. "I will try the door."

In a moment he was back. "It is open," he whispered.

"Kepta believes," mused Thrala, "that we will keep to the safety of the gallery. Therefore let us go through the pit. The morgels will be gone to better hunting grounds."

Through the pit they went. A choking stench arose from underfoot and they trod very carefully. They climbed the stairs on the far side unchallenged, Dandtan leading.

"The rod here, Garin," he called; "this door is barred."

Garin pressed the weapon into the other's hand and leaned against the rock. He was sick and dizzy. The long, deep wounds on his arm and shoulder were stiffening and ached with a biting throb.

When they went on he panted with effort. They still moved in darkness and his distress passed unnoticed.

"This is wrong," he muttered, half to himself. "We go too easily—"

And he was answered out of the blackness. "Well noted, outlander. But you go free for the moment, as does Thrala and Dandtan. Our full accounting is not yet. And now, farewell, until we meet again in the Hall of Thrones. I could find it in me to applaud your courage, outlander. Perhaps you will come to serve me yet."

Garin turned and threw himself toward the voice, bringing up with bruising force against rock wall. Kepta laughed.

"Not with the skill of the bull Tand will you capture me."

His second laugh was cut cleanly off, as if a door had been closed. In silence the three hurried up the ramp. Then, as through a curtain, they came into the light of Tav.

Thrala let fall her drab cloak, stood with arms outstretched in the crater land. Her sparkling robe sheathed her in glory and she sang softly, rapt in her own delight. Then Dandtan put his arm about her; she clung to him, staring about as might a beauty-bewildered child.

Garin wondered dully how he would be able to make the journey back to the Caverns when his arm and shoulder were eaten with a consuming fire. The Ana crept closer to him, peering into his white face.

They were aroused by a howl from the Caves. Thrala cried out and Dandtan answered her unspoken question. "They have set the morgels on our trail!"

The howl from the Caves was echoed from the forest. Morgels before and behind them! Garin might set himself against one, Dandtan another, and Thrala could defend herself with the rod, but in the end the pack would kill them.

"We shall claim protection from the Gibi of the cliff. By the law they must give us aid," said Thrala, as, turning up her long robe, she began to run lightly. Garin picked up her cloak and drew it across his shoulder to hide his welts. When he could no longer hold her pace she must not guess the reason for his falling behind.

Of that flight through the forest the flyer afterward remembered little. At last the gurgle of water broke upon his pounding ears, as he stumbled along a good ten lengths behind his companions. They had come to the edge of the wood along the banks of the river.

Without hesitation Thrala and Dandtan plunged into the oily flood, swimming easily for the other side. Garin dropped the cloak, wondering if, once he stepped into the yellow stream, he would ever be able to struggle out again. Already the Ana was in, paddling in circles near the shore and pleading with him to follow. Wearily Garin waded out.

The water, which washed the blood and sweat from his aching body, was faintly brackish and stung his wounds to life. He could not fight the sluggish current and it bore him downstream, well away from where the others landed.

But at last he managed to win free, crawling out near where a smaller stream joined the river. There he lay panting, face down upon the moss. And there they found him, water dripping from his bedraggled finery, the Ana stroking his muddied hair. Thrala cried out with concern and pillowed his head on her knees while Dandtan examined his wounds.

"Why did you not tell us?" demanded Thrala.

He did not try to answer, content to lie there, her arms supporting him. Dandtan disappeared into the forest, returning soon, his hands filled with a mass of crushed leaves. With these he plastered Garin's wounds.

"You'd better go on," Garin warned.

Dandtan shook his head. "The morgels can not swim. If they cross, they must go to the bridge, and that is half the crater away."

The Ana dropped into their midst, its small hands filled with clusters of purple fruit. And so they feasted, Garin at ease on a fern couch, accepting food from Thrala's hand.

There seemed to be some virtue in Dandtan's leaf plaster for, after a short rest, Garin was able to get to his feet with no more than a twinge or two in his wounds. But they started on at a more sober pace. Through mossy glens and sunlit glades where strange flowers made perfume, the trail led. The stream they followed branched twice before, on the edge of meadow land, they struck away from the guiding water toward the crater wall.

Suddenly Thrala threw back her head and gave a shrill, sweet whistle. Out of the air dropped a yellow and black insect, as large as a hawk. Twice it circled her head and then perched itself on her outstretched wrist.

Its swollen body was jet black, its curving legs, three to a side, chrome yellow. The round head ended in a sharp beak and it had large, many-faceted eyes. The wings, which lazily tested the air, were black and touched with gold.

Thrala rubbed the round head while the insect nuzzled affectionately at her cheek. Then she held out her wrist again and it was gone.

"We shall be expected now and may pass unmolested."

Shortly they became aware of a murmuring sound. The crater wall loomed ahead, dwarfing the trees at its base.

"There is the city of the Gibi," remarked Dandtan.

Clinging to the rock were the towers and turrets of many eight-sided cells.

"They are preparing for the Mists," observed Thrala. "We shall have company on our journey to the Caverns."

They passed the trees and reached the foot of the wax skyscrapers which towered dizzily above their heads. A great cloud of the Gibi hovered about them. Garin felt the soft brush of their wings against his body. And they crowded each other jealously to be near Thrala.

The soft *hush-hush* of their wings filled the clearing as one large Gibi of outstanding beauty approached. The commoners fluttered off and Thrala greeted the Queen of the cells as an equal. Then she turned to her companions with the information the Gibi Queen had to offer.

"We are just in time. Tomorrow the Gibi leave. The morgels have crossed the river and are out of control. Instead of hunting us they have gone to ravage the forest lands. All Tav has been warned against them. But they may be caught by the Mist and so destroyed. We are to rest in the cliff hollows, and one shall come for us when it is time to leave."

The Gibi withdrew to the cell-combs after conducting their guests to the rock-hollows.

Chapter 9 Days of Preparation

Garin was awakened by a loud murmuring. Dandtan knelt beside him.

"We must go. Even now the Gibi seal the last of the cells."

They ate hurriedly of cakes of grain and honey, and, as they feasted, the Queen again visited them. The first of the swarm were already winging eastward.

With the Gibi nation hanging like a storm cloud above them, the three started off across the meadow. The purple-blue haze was thickening and, here and there, curious formations, like the dust devils of the desert, arose and danced and disappeared again. The tropic heat of Tav increased; it was as if the ground itself were steaming.

"The Mists draw close; we must hurry," panted Dandtan.

They traversed the tongue of forest which bordered the meadow and came to the central plain of Tav. There was a brooding stillness there. The Ana, perched on Garin's shoulder, shivered.

Their walk became a trot; the Gibi bunched together. Once Thrala caught her breath in a half sob.

"They are flying slowly because of us. And it's so far—"

"Look!" Dandtan pointed at the plain. "The morgels!"

The morgel pack, driven by fear, ran in leaping bounds. They passed within a hundred yards of the three, yet did not turn from their course, though several snarled at them.

"They are already dead," observed Dandtan. "There is no time for them to reach the shelter of the Caves."

Splashing through a shallow brook, the three began to run. For the first time Thrala faltered and broke pace. Garin thrust the Ana into Dandtan's arms and, before she could protest, swept the girl into his arms.

The haze was denser now, settling upon them as a curtain. Black hair, finer than silk, whipped across Garin's throat. Thrala's head was on his shoulder, her heaving breasts arched as she gasped the sultry air.

"They—keep—watch… !" shouted Dandtan.

Piercing the gloom were pin-points of light. A dark shape grazed Garin's head—one of the Gibi Queen's guards.

Then abruptly they stumbled into a throng of the Folk, one of whom reached for Thrala with a crooning cry. It was Sera welcoming her mistress.

Thrala was borne away by the women, leaving Garin with a feeling of desolation.

"The Mists, Outlander." It was Urg, pointing toward the Cavern mouth. Two of the Folk swung their weight on a lever. Across the opening a sheet of crystal clicked into place. The Caverns were sealed.

The haze was now inky black outside and billows of it beat against the protecting barrier. It might have been midnight of the blackest, starless night.

"So will it be for forty days. What is without—dies," said Urg.

"Then we have forty days in which to prepare," Garin spoke his thought aloud. Dandtan's keen face lightened.

"Well said, Garin. Forty days before Kepta may seek us. And we have much to do. But first, our respects to the Lord of the Folk."

Together they went to the Hall of Thrones where, when he saw Dandtan, Trar arose and held out his jade-tipped rod of office. The son of the Ancient Ones touched it.

"Hail! Dweller in the Light, and Outlander who has fulfilled the promise of Thran. Thrala is once more within the Caverns. Now send you to dust this black throne... ."

Garin, nothing loath, drew the destroying rod from his belt, but Dandtan shook his head. "The time is not yet, Trar. Kepta must finish the pattern he began. Forty days have we and then the Black Ones come."

Trar considered thoughtfully. "So that be the way of it. Thran did not see another war... ."

"But he saw an end to Kepta!"

Trar straightened as if some burden had rolled from his thin shoulders. "Well do you speak, Lord. When there is one to sit upon the Rose Throne, what have we to fear? Listen, O ye Folk, the Light has returned to the Caverns!"

His cry was echoed by the gathering of the Folk.

"And now, Lord—" he turned to Dandtan with deference— "what are your commands?"

"For the space of one sleep I shall enter the Chamber of Renewing with this outlander, who is no longer an outlander but one, Garin, accepted by the Daughter according to the Law. And while we rest let all be made ready… ."

"The Dweller in the Light has spoken!" Trar himself escorted them from the Hall.

They came, through many winding passages, to a deep pool of water, in the depths of which lurked odd purple shadows. Dandtan stripped and plunged in, Garin following his example. The water was tinglingly alive and they did not linger in it long. From it they went to a bubble room such as the one Garin had rested in after the bath of light rays, and on the cushions in its center stretched their tired bodies.

When Garin awoke he experienced the same exultation he had felt before. Dandtan regarded him with a smile. "Now to work," he said, as he reached out to press a knob set in the wall.

Two of the Folk appeared, bringing with them clean trappings. After they dressed and broke their fast, Dandtan started for the laboratories. Garin would have gone with him, but Sera intercepted them.

"There is one would speak with Lord Garin… ."

Dandtan laughed. "Go," he ordered the American. "Thrala's commands may not be slighted."

The Hall of Women was deserted. And the corridor beyond, roofed and walled with slabs of rose-shot crystal, was as empty. Sera drew aside a golden curtain and they were in the audience chamber of the Daughter.

A semi-circular dais of the clearest crystal, heaped with rose and gold cushions, faced them. Before it, a fountain, in the form of a flower nodding on a curved stem, sent a spray of water into a shallow basin. The walls of the room were divided into alcoves by marble pillars, each one curved in semblance of a fern frond.

From the domed ceiling, on chains of twisted gold, seven lamps, each wrought from a single yellow sapphire, gave soft light. The floor was a mosaic of gold and crystal.

Two small Anas, who had been playing among the cushions, pattered up to exchange greetings with Garin's. But of the mistress of the chamber there was no sign. Garin turned to Sera, but before he could phrase his question, she asked mockingly:

"Who is the Lord Garin that he can not wait with patience?" But she left in search of the Daughter.

Garin glanced uneasily about the room. This jeweled chamber was no place for him. He had started toward the door when

Thrala stepped within.

"Greetings to the Daughter." His voice sounded formal and cold, even to himself.

Her hands, which had been outheld in welcome, dropped to her sides. A ghost of a frown dimmed her beauty.

"Greetings, Garin," she returned slowly.

"You sent for me—" he prompted, eager to escape from this jewel box and the unattainable treasure it held.

"Yes," the coldness of her tone was an order of exile. "I would know how you fared and whether your wounds yet troubled you."

He looked down at his own smooth flesh, cleanly healed by the wisdom of the Folk. "I am myself again and eager to be at such work as Dandtan can find for me... ."

Her robe seemed to hiss across the floor as she turned upon him. "Then go!" she ordered. "Go quickly!"

And blindly he obeyed. She had spoken as if to a servant, one whom she could summon and dismiss by whim. Even if Dandtan held her love, she might have extended him her friendship. But he knew within him that friendship would be a poor crumb beside the feast his pulses pounded for.

There was a pattering of feet behind him. So, she would call him back! His pride sent him on. But it was Sera. Her head thrust forward until she truly resembled a reptile.

"Fool! Morgel!" she spat. "Even the Black Ones did not treat her so. Get you out of the Place of Women lest they divide your skin among them!"

Garin broke free, not heeding her torrent of reproach. Then he seized upon one of the Folk as a guide and sought the laboratories. Far beneath the surface of Tav, where the light-motes shone ghostly in the gloom, they came into a place of ceaseless activity, where there were tables crowded with instruments, coils of glass and metal tubing, and other equipment and supplies. These were the focusing point for ceaseless streams of the Folk. On a platform at the far end, Garin saw the tall son of the Ancient Ones working on a framework of metal and shining crystal.

He glanced up as Garin joined him. "You are late," he accused. "But your excuse is a good one. Now get you to work. Hold this here—and here—while I fasten these clamps."

So Garin became extra hands and feet for Dandtan, and they

worked feverishly to build against the lifting of the Mists. There was no day or night in the laboratories. They worked steadily without rest, and without feeling fatigue.

Twice they went to the Chamber of Renewing, but except for these trips to the upper ways they were not out of the laboratories through all those days. Of Thrala there was no sign, nor did any one speak of her.

The Cavern dwellers were depending upon two defenses: an evil green liquid, to be thrown in frail glass globes, and a screen charged with energy. Shortly before the lifting of the Mists, these arms were transported to the entrance and installed there. Dandtan and Garin made a last inspection.

"Kepta makes the mistake of under-rating his enemies," Dandtan reflected, feeling the edge of the screen caressingly. "When I was captured, on the day my people died, I was sent to the Black Ones' laboratories so that their seekers after knowledge might learn the secrets of the Ancient Ones. But I proved a better pupil than teacher and I discovered the defense against the Black Fire. After I had learned that, Kepta grew impatient with my supposed stupidity and tried to use me to force Thrala to his will. For that, as for other things, shall he pay—and the paying will not be in coin of his own striking. Let us think of that... ." He turned to greet Urg and Trar and the other leaders of the Folk, who had approached unnoticed.

Among them stood Thrala, her gaze fixed upon the crystal wall between them and the thinning Mist. She noticed Garin no more than she did the Anas playing with her train and the women whispering behind her. But Garin stepped back into the shadows— and what he saw was not weapons of war, but cloudy black hair and graceful white limbs veiled in splendor.

Urg and one of the other chieftains bore down upon the door lever. With a protesting squeak, the glass wall disappeared into the rock. The green of Tav beckoned them out to walk in its freshness; it was renewed with lusty life. But in all that expanse of meadow and forest there was a strange stillness.

"Post sentries," ordered Dandtan. "The Black Ones will come soon."

He beckoned Garin forward as he spoke to Thrala:

"Let us go to the Hall of Thrones."

But the Daughter did not answer his smile. "It is not meet that we should spend time in idle talk. Let us go instead to call upon the help of those who have gone before us." So speaking, she darted a glance at Garin as chill as the arctic lands beyond the lip of Tav, and then swept away with Sera bearing her train.

Dandtan stared at Garin. "What has happened between you two?"

The flyer shook his head. "I don't know. No man is born with an understanding of women—"

"But she is angered with you. What has happened?"

For a moment Garin was tempted to tell the truth: that he dared not break any barrier she chose to raise, lest he seize what in honor was none of his. But he shook his head mutely. Neither of them saw Thrala again until Death entered the Caverns.

Chapter 10 Battle and Victory

Garin stood with Dandtan looking out into the plain of Tav. Some distance away were two slender, steel-tipped towers, which were, in reality, but hollow tubes filled with the Black Fire. Before these dark-clad figures were busy.

"They seem to believe us already defeated. Let them think so," commented Dandtan, touching the screen they had erected before the Cavern entrance.

As he spoke Kepta swaggered through the tall grass to call a greeting:

"Ho, rock dweller, I would speak with you—"

Dandtan edged around the screen, Garin a pace behind.

"I see you, Kepta."

"Good. I trust that your ears will serve you as well as your eyes. These are my terms: Give Thrala to me to dwell in my chamber and the outlander to provide sport for my captains. Make no resistance but throw open the Caverns so that I may take my rightful place in the Hall of Thrones. Do this and we shall be at peace... ."

"And this is our reply:"—Dandtan stood unmovingly before the screen—"Return to the Caves; break down the bridge between your land and ours. Let no Black One come hither again, ever... ."

Kepta laughed. "So, that be the way of it! Then this shall we do: take Thrala, to be mine for a space, and then to go to my captains—"

Garin hurled himself forward, felt Kepta's lips mash beneath his fist; his fingers were closing about the other's throat as Dandtan, who was trying to pull him away from his prey, shouted a warning: "Watch out!"

A morgel had leaped from the grass, its teeth snapping about Garin's wrist, forcing him to drop Kepta. Then Dandtan laid it senseless by a sharp blow with his belt.

On hands and knees Kepta crawled back to his men. The lower part of his face was a red and dripping smear. He screamed an order with savage fury.

Dandtan drew the still raging flyer behind the screen. "Be a little prudent," he panted. "Kepta can be dealt with in other ways than with bare hands."

The towers were swinging their tips toward the entrance.

Dandtan ordered the screen wedged tightly into place.

Outside, the morgel Dandtan had stunned got groggily to its feet. When it had limped half the distance back to its master, Kepta gave the order to fire. The broad beam of black light from the tip of the nearest tower caught the beast head on. There was a chilling scream of agony, and where the morgel had stood gray ashes drifted on the wind.

A hideous crackling arose as the black beam struck the screen. Green grass beneath seared away, leaving only parched earth and naked blue soil. Those within the Cavern crouched behind their frail protection, half blinded by the light from the seared grass, coughing from the chemical-ridden fumes which curled about the cracks of the rock.

Then the beam faded out. Thin smoke plumed from the tips of the towers, steam arose from the blackened ground. Dandtan drew a deep breath.

"It held!" he cried, betraying at last the fear which had ridden him.

Men of the Folk dragged engines of tubing before the screen, while others brought forth the globes of green liquid. Dandtan stood aside, as if this matter were the business of the Folk alone, and Garin recalled that the Ancient Ones were opposed to the taking of life.

Trar was in command now. At his orders the globes were posed on spoon-shaped holders. Loopholes in the screen clicked open. Trar brought down his hand in signal. The globes arose lazily, sliding through the loopholes and floating out toward the towers.

One, aimed short, struck the ground where the fire had burned it bare, and broke. The liquid came forth, sluggishly, forming a gray-green gas as the air struck it. Another spiral of gas arose almost at the foot of one of the towers—and then another ... and another.

There quickly followed a tortured screaming, which soon dwindled to a weak yammering. They could see shapes, no longer human or animal, staggering about in the fog.

Dandtan turned away, his face white with horror. Garin's hands were over his ears to shut out that crying.

At last it was quiet; there was no more movement by the towers. Urg placed a sphere of rosy light upon the nearest machine and flipped it out into the camp of the enemy. As if it were a magnet it drew the green tendrils of gas, to leave the air clear. Here and there lay shrunken, livid shapes, the towers brooding over them.

One of the Folk burst into their midst, a woman of Thrala's following.

"Haste!" She clawed at Garin. "Kepta takes Thrala!"

She ran wildly back the way she had come, with the American pounding at her heels. They burst into the Hall of Thrones and saw a struggling group before the dais.

Garin heard someone howl like an animal, became aware the sound came from his own throat. For the second time his fist found its mark on Kepta's face. With a shriek of rage the Black One threw Thrala from him and sprang at Garin, his nails tearing gashes in the flyer's face. Twice the American twisted free and sent bone-crushing blows into the other's ribs. Then he got the grip he wanted, and his fingers closed around Kepta's throat. In spite of the Black One's struggles he held on until a limp body rolled beneath him.

Panting, the American pulled himself up from the blood-stained floor and grabbed the arm of the Jade Throne for support.

"Garin!" Thrala's arms were about him, her pitying fingers on his wounds. And in that moment he forgot Dandtan, forgot everything he had steeled himself to remember. She was in his arms and his mouth sought hers possessively. Nor was she unresponsive, but yielded, as a flower yields to the wind.

"Garin!" she whispered softly. Then, almost shyly, she broke from his hold.

Beyond her stood Dandtan, his face white, his mouth tight. Garin remembered. And, a little mad with pain and longing, he dropped his eyes, trying not to see the loveliness which was Thrala.

"So, Outlander, Thrala flies to your arms—"

Garin whirled about. Kepta was hunched on the broad seat of the jet throne.

"No, I am not dead, Outlander—nor shall you kill me, as you think to do. I go now, but I shall return. We have met and hated, fought and died before—you and I. You were a certain Garan, Marshall of the air fleet of Yu-Lac on a vanished world, and I was Lord of Koom. That was in the days before the Ancient Ones pioneered space. You and I and Thrala, we are bound together and even fate can not break those bonds. Farewell, Garin. And do you, Thrala, remember the ending of that other Garan. It was not an easy one."

With a last malicious chuckle, he leaned back in the throne.

His battered body slumped. Then the sharp lines of the throne blurred; it shimmered in the light. Abruptly then both it and its occupant were gone. They were staring at empty space, above which loomed the rose throne of the Ancient Ones.

"He spoke true," murmured Thrala. "We have had other lives, other meetings—so will we meet again. But for the present he returns to the darkness which sent him forth. It is finished."

Without warning, a low rumbling filled the Cavern; the walls rocked and swayed. Lizard and human, they huddled together until the swaying stopped. Finally a runner appeared with news that one of the Gibi had ventured forth and discovered that the Caves of Darkness had been sealed by an underground quake. The menace of the Black Ones was definitely at an end.

Chapter 11 Thrala's Mate

Although there were falls of rock within the Caverns and some of the passages were closed, few of the Folk suffered injury. Gibi scouts reported that the land about the entrance to the Caves had sunk, and that the River of Gold, thrown out of its bed, was fast filling this basin to form a lake.

As far as they could discover, none of the Black Ones had survived the battle and the sealing of the Caves. But they could not be sure that there was not a handful of outlaws somewhere within the confines of Tav.

The Crater itself was changed. A series of raw hills had appeared in the central plain. The pool of boiling mud had vanished and trees in the forest lay flat, as if cut by a giant scythe.

Upon their return to the cliff city, the Gibi found most of their wax skyscrapers in ruins, but they set about rebuilding without complaint. The squirrel farmers emerged from their burrows and were again busy in the fields.

Garin felt out of place in all the activity that filled the Caverns. More than ever he was the outlander with no true roots in Tav. Restlessly, he explored the Caverns, spending many hours in the Place of Ancestors, where he studied those men of the outer world who had preceded him into this weird land.

One night when he came back to his chamber he found Dandtan and Trar awaiting him there. There was a curious hardness in Dandtan's attitude, a somber sobriety in Trar's carriage.

"Have you sought the Hall of Women since the battle?" demanded the son of the Ancient Ones abruptly.

"No," retorted Garin shortly. Did Dandtan accuse him of double dealing?

"Have you sent a message to Thrala?"

Garin held back his rising temper. "I have not ventured where I can not."

Dandtan nodded to Trar as if his suspicions had been confirmed. "You see how it stands, Trar."

Trar shook his head slowly. "But never has the summoning been at fault—"

"You forget," Dandtan reminded him sharply. "It was once— and the penalty was exacted. So shall it be again."

Garin looked from one to the other, confused. Dandtan seemed possessed of a certain ruthless anger, but Trar was manifestly unhappy.

"It must come after council, the Daughter willing," the Lord of the Folk said.

Dandtan strode toward the door. "Thrala is not to know. Assemble the Council tonight. Meanwhile, see that he," he jerked his thumb toward Garin, "does not leave this room."

Thus Garin became a prisoner under the guard of the Folk, unable to discover of what Dandtan accused him, or how he had aroused the hatred of the Cavern ruler. Unless Dandtan's jealousy had been aroused and he was determined to rid himself of a rival.

Believing this, the flyer went willingly to the chamber where the judges waited. Dandtan sat at the head of a long table, Trar at his right hand and lesser nobles of the Folk beyond.

"You know the charge," Dandtan's words were tipped with venom as Garin came to stand before him. "Out of his own mouth has this outlander condemned himself. Therefore I ask that you decree for him the fate of that outlander of the second calling who rebelled against the summoning."

"The outlander has admitted his fault?" questioned one of the Folk.

Trar inclined his head sadly. "He did."

As Garin opened his mouth to demand a stating of the charge against him, Dandtan spoke again:

"What say you, Lords?"

For a long moment they sat in silence and then they bobbed their lizard heads in assent. "Do as you desire, Dweller in the Light."

Dandtan smiled without mirth. "Look, outlander." He passed his hand over the glass of the seeing mirror set in the table top. "This is the fate of him who rebels—"

In the shining surface Garin saw pictured a break in Tav's wall. At its foot stood a group of men of the Ancient Ones, and in their midst struggled a prisoner. They were forcing him to climb the crater wall. Garin watched him reach the lip and crawl over, to stagger across the steaming rock, dodging the scalding vapor of hot springs, until he pitched face down in the slimy mud.

"Such was his ending, and so will you end—"

The calm brutality of that statement aroused Garin's anger. "Rather would I die that way than linger in this den," he cried hotly.

"You, who owe your life to me, would send me to such a death without even telling me of what I am accused. Little is there to choose between you and Kepta, after all—except that he was an open enemy!"

Dandtan sprang to his feet, but Trar caught his arm.

"He speaks fairly. Ask him why he will not fulfill the summoning."

While Dandtan hesitated, Garin leaned across the table, flinging his words, weapon-like, straight into that cold face.

"I'll admit that I love Thrala—have loved her since that moment when I saw her on the steps of the morgel pit in the caves. Since when has it become a crime to love that which may not be yours—if you do not try to take it?"

Trar released Dandtan, his golden eyes gleaming.

"If you love her, claim her. It is your right."

"Do I not know," Garin turned to him, "that she is Dandtan's. Thran had no idea of Dandtan's survival when he laid his will upon her. Shall I stoop to holding her to an unwelcome bargain? Let her go to the one she loves... ."

Dandtan's face was livid, and his hands, resting on the table, trembled. One by one the lords of the Folk slipped away, leaving the two face-to-face.

"And I thought to order you to your death." Dandtan's whisper was husky as it emerged between dry lips. "Garin, we thought you knew—and, knowing, had refused her."

"Knew what?"

"That I am Thran's son—and Thrala's brother."

The floor swung beneath Garin's unsteady feet. Dandtan's hands were warm on his shoulders.

"I am a fool," said the American slowly.

Dandtan smiled. "A very honorable fool! Now get you to Thrala, who deserves to hear the full of this tangle."

So it was that, with Dandtan by his side, Garin walked for the second time down that hallway, to pass the golden curtains and stand in the presence of the Daughter. She came straight from her cushions into his arms when she read what was in his face. They needed no words.

And in that hour began Garin's life in Tav.

Made in the USA
Monee, IL
09 December 2022

20489039R00031